TALLOW

A JOURNEY OF A CHAMPION

SCOTT RISCH

The Tallow Trilogy Book One

TotalRecall Publications, Inc.
1103 Middlecreek
Friendswood, Texas 77546
281-992-3131 TEL
www.TotalRecallPress.com

ISBN: 978-1-64883-082-2
UPC: 6-43977-40822-8
Library of Congress Control Number: 2021935894

FIRST EDITION
1   2   3   4   5   6   7   8   9   10

Dedication

This book is dedicated to all those who try to do the right thing, for God, with their words and with their lives. Don't get discouraged when what is right goes against what your pride or what the people around you say. My pastor used to always say, "It's never wrong to do right, and it's never right to do wrong." In my opinion, God blesses those whose motivation is to do right for Him.

The thoughts of the righteous are right: but the counsels of the wicked are deceit.

--Proverbs 12:5 (KJV)

When a man's ways please the Lord, he maketh even his enemies to be at peace with him.

--Proverbs 16:7 (KJV)

Table of Contents

Chapter 1

The Little Champion

The boy walked down the market street as the salty breeze of the coastline invaded his senses. His brown curls bounced all around his head with the excitement of a nine-year-old. He was twining a bead chain with his fingers when a booming voice startled him.

"Fresh fish!" A heavy-set man, draped in a fine robe, called out. In his servant's hand was a large fish, still wiggling from the catch of the day. The boy ducked to keep from being slapped by the fish's tail.

"I can see that you are a man of great taste." Another voice chimed. "May I interest you in some jewelry that makes the others pale in comparison?" The boy rolled his eyes and hurried off to the blacksmith shop. This town always amazed him with new merchants coming in and going out on the ships of the Caesarean shoreline.

He slowly approached his father, who was banging and shaping a piece of red-hot metal. No matter how many times he'd walked around, he seemed to always find something new in his father's shop.

"What's this?" The boy asked as he picked up an obscure piece of metal.

"I'm glad that you asked. That is the rest of this." His father said as he lifted a large wooden shield from the ground.

Instantly the boy could see where the metal piece in his hand went on the shield. He snapped the piece into the cut grooves and his father patted his shoulder.

"That's right, Tallow my boy." He chuckled. "I knew this would rub onto you some day."

Tallow handed him the burlap sack his mother gave him.

"What's this?" His father asked as he felt the sack.

"It's lunch." Tallow said with a shrug of his shoulders.

"Where did your mother get Ostrich eggs?" He uncovered the loaves from the burlap. "Don't tell her I said that." He said with a blush and Tallow grinned.

"Son. Will you take the bucket and get some water from the well?"

The knock of the bread on the table answered Tallow's question. The water wasn't just for drinking.

Tallow returned with the water and saw his father admiring his own workmanship in the shield before him.

"Come here, my boy."

Tallow eagerly ran to his father's side.

"Stand here."

The boy stood up straight in an attention stance and looked up as a shadow passed over him.

The trunk armor his father dropped onto his shoulders made him stumble back.

"Stick out your arm." His father chuckled.

The forearm shield swallowed his arm as its weight made his body sag.

"Some day, my boy. Some day." His father said with a dreamy look in his eyes.

"Run along now. I've got work to do for Caesar's men." He

said with a devilish grin. He turned and winked at Tallow as he lifted the iron shell from the boy's body. Tallow smiled and ran outside.

A distant yelping caught his attention as he trotted down the street. His stride quickened when he heard boys' laughter passing in the same direction.

Tallow grabbed two sticks from a pup tent on the way. He slapped a rock filled hand and cracked a laughing head in one motion.

"Get him!" A defiant high-pitched voice commanded.

Tallow bolted through the marketplace as he heard the rocks crash behind him. He made his way through to a rocky plateau on the edge of town. He found a huge stone nestled in a rock wall pocket to make his stand.

The boys approached him with cocky, smiling faces, like a pack of wolves to a dying lamb. They flipped their rocks playfully between their hands with arrogant confidence.

"Now we have a bigger target to play with." The same whiney voice from the marketplace cracked. He stepped out from the pack. His face was pudgy, and it overshadowed a chubby frame that held a rock for the battle ahead.

Tallow defied his threat with a thrust of his arms, crossing his sticks in an "X" pattern.

The boy scowled and hurled the stone with all his might. Tallow answered by batting the rock into another clutched hand. One by one, the gang of boys curled back and whimpered away after being struck by their own rocks. Parents, who heard the flurry, grabbed their boys and glared at Tallow as they hurried off.

He stood alone on the rock and his body began to relax at the sight of the boys leaving. His hand reached to rub an itch on his cheek and returned with blood tipped fingers.

"Come here boy." The gruff voice of a Roman soldier called.

Tallow crept down from the rock, trying not to look the man in the face. It was hard to get around the soldier's mountainous shadow, but he swallowed hard and stood at his feet.

With a soft gesture the man cupped the child's chin in his hand and said, "You've done nothing wrong boy. You handled yourself well."

A shy smile crept back on to Tallow's face as the soldier smiled back.

"What's your name, son? Where do you live?" He scooped Tallow up and flipped him onto his shoulders before he could answer.

"My name is Tallow." He said giggling. "I'm the Blacksmith's son."

The soldier tickled and wrestled with the boy all the way to his house. He made him laugh and his fear soon turned into friendship. The soldier's name was Darius and he took great interest in Tallow from that day on.

When the two reached the Blacksmith's shop, the soldier flipped Tallow back to the ground.

"Run along now. Your father and I have some things to discuss.

Those words worried Tallow and his face showed it.

"Remember what I said, boy." Darius bent to face Tallow. "It wasn't your fault.

With that the boy turned and walked out the door. He wasn't really convinced of his own innocence, but he took Darius' word for it.

The soldier turned to Barsiebus, who was glaring at him.

"What's this about?" Tallow's father blurted out.

Darius was irritated, but calm. "Friend, I know he's your boy, but don't get defensive yet. My name is Darius and I'd like to know more about the boy.

"Well, uh…." Darius hesitated.

"Barsiebus." Tallow's father said as he reluctantly stuck his hand out.

"Barsiebus. Your boy, Tallow, walloped about five or six of the village brats in defense of a mongrel dog today. They had rocks and all he had was two sticks, but he sent them home to their mothers." Darius told Barsiebus all that happened that afternoon.

"I'm almost sure that I've seen his style of swordplay in some of the Asian provinces."

"He was born in the shade of a Chinese Tallow tree." Tallow's mother interrupted with a pitcher of water for her guest.

"That's where I learned my trade as a blacksmith, from a man named Hwang To. He was bigger than me, but gentle as a lamb and patient. Oh, I'm sorry, this is my wife, Rachael." Barsiebus jumped up and waved his hand in her direction.

Darius rose to his feet and nodded his head in her direction smiling. "Ma'am, it's good that I met you both. I have one more question. How old is the boy?"

"He's barely nine." Rachael panicked. She knew Rome would take her son to be a soldier.

"Barely nine?" Barsiebus laughed. "His birthday was seven months ago.

"He's incredibly sound for a boy his age." Darius stated.

"That's his mother's fault." Barsiebus said as he winked at his wife.

"Barsiebus, don't be too hard on the boy. He was doing the right thing. Those boys deserved what they got." With an approving nod from Barsiebus, Darius turned and walked out.

Tallow didn't have any close friends in this village and after what had happened today, he was sure that he didn't have a chance at getting any. A wet muzzle on his hand said he had at least one. It was the dog from the marketplace. A set of big brown eyes blinked at him from a matted coat of caramel colored hair. The dog was holding one leg up gingerly and balancing on the other three.

Tallow looked at the injured leg. "Easy boy. I won't hurt you."

He was relieved to see that the wound didn't go all the way through. He got some fresh water and clean rags from his father's shop and dressed the leg as best as he could.

"Is this the one you were the 'hero' for today?" His father asked him from behind.

"Uh…Yes, Sir. There was a hole in his leg, so I cleaned it up." Tallow said, pointing to the ragged bandage.

"Give him these." His father handed him a pan of spongy rolls from the morning. "If you tell your mother, I'll deny it." His father winked at him.

Tallow set the pan in front of the dog. It hoisted itself onto three legs and lapped at the mixture.

"Tallow. The dog will be fine. We have some things to discuss."

Tallow cringed with those words as his shoulders dropped down with embarrassment.

"Don't get so glum. The soldier….Darius, is it?" The boy nodded. "said you handled yourself quite well today. He was very impressed with your 'swordplay', as he called it. He told me everything and I believe as he does. Those boys deserved what you gave them and more. I just wish I could've been there to see it."

Tallow's face exposed a sheepish grin.

"He said that he would be keeping his eyes on you, not just for your protection. He said that you will be warrior worthy in a few years.

Tallow spoke his thoughts. "Me? A warrior? I was just trying not to get hit. I didn't mean to hurt anybody. I just got lucky. Those boys weren't really trying and…" His thoughts were racing as his father brought them to a halt.

"Maybe news of this will get to Caesar. That couldn't hurt your future.

From the expression on his face, Tallow could tell his father was stuck in his dream again. He wasn't sure if he wanted to be stuck in the same dream as his father or not.

Dreams may come and go, but Tallow's life would soon be changed drastically. Caesar's ears were filled with 'Tallow' more than once.

News of the fight traveled throughout the whole Roman garrison. More soldiers were stopping by his father's shop to inspect his goods. His friend Darius had seen enough commotion about the boy and decided to have a talk with his captain.

"Captain, I request an audience with you."

"Why so formal, Darius? You know my door is always open to you." Malcus said with a little irritation.

"It is because the request I have is a formal one."

"I'm listening."

"Can you ask the men not to *patrol* the market so much?"

"What do we need of patrols? Is there a faction that they need to put down?"

"No. They just want to gawk at the boy, 'Tallow'.

"Well, your tale of the boy's fight made everyone a little inquisitive. I was planning to go by and see the blacksmith myself later today and…"

"Please, Captain, don't do that. Let the boy breathe a little bit. The stories I've heard in the market are much larger than the one I told you, ranging from the sticks he used being elephant's tusks, to the rocks being great boulders. I'm not saying to forget about the boy, but so many stories of such magnitude are hard for anyone to live up to."

"Yes. It would be better to have a willing servant of Caesar, rather than a begrudging ally. I see your point."

"Thank you, Captain. You won't regret it." He said as he turned toward the door.

"We'll take the boy in the summer of his eleventh year."

That comment stunned Darius as he turned back around.

"Surely you don't think it was just my skills in the field that made me Captain. I have ears in the market as well."

Darius turned back and shook his head as he walked out.

Chapter 2

The Conflict Begins

The sun pierced the boy's eyelids, causing him to squint. He was no longer the scrawny little hero that everyone whispered about in the marketplace. A year and a half of blacksmith work had indeed changed his physical appearance. He lifted his short stocky frame from his bed and stretched to get the blood flowing.

"Time to wake up! You dogs of Caesar!" A man barked while throwing water on the sleepers and ignoring those standing.

Tallow fell in line with the others as they slowly rambled down the aisl.

"Well, look what the dog threw up." A vaguely familiar voice chided.

As Tallow turned, the pudgy little boy from the marketplace now towered over him. His face and shirt were wet from being doused with water.

"I'll see you in the dirt before the day ends." The boy threatened.

"Why wait for dirt?" Tallow brought up his knee with such force; it lifted the oaf from his feet. Tallow then stepped casually back in line as the boy lay doubled-over and squirming behind him.

The man with the water came rushing over to see what the excitement was about. The boys separated to reveal the grimacing lump before them. A knowing smile crept onto the man's face. He tried to be stern and not laugh.

"Get up boy. They'll grow back."

Tallow joined the now snickering crowd, but he knew that this wasn't the end. This one would be coming back for more.

*****

Darius passed the Clarion Board just as the matches were being posted. His anxious hands couldn't snatch the list from the board fast enough.

"Who gave you this list, boy?"

With an irritated scowl the boy said. "I'm fifteen and it was Captain Malcus."

"Check your tone boy, before I feed you your teeth!"

"Yes sir." He squelched his indignation. "Sir."

"Yes."

"Captain Malcus knew you wouldn't approve. He told me that he wants a word with you."

"Oh. I'll give him more words than he wants." Darius muttered.

"Sir?"

"You've delivered your message, now go about your business."

"Yes Sir."

"He's not training soldiers, he's raising game cocks." His thoughts raged on. *"This boy towers over him by at least a forearm length. Oh, well. Let's see what the good Captain has to say."*

Tallow could hear the clash of shields and swords as he entered the arena. The smell of sweat from man and beast tainted every breath as he walked past knowing and suspicious eyes. Captains barked out orders as they cursed their students for imperfections. His eyes scanned the crowd for a familiar face, other than the one he saw this morning.

Darius looked up from his soldiers to give Tallow a quick, approving nod before rejoining the conversation.

"Hello." A voice came from Tallow's side.

He turned and saw a shy smile on a skinny head beside him. "What are you looking at?!" Tallow blurted out.

"I was just being friendly!" The shy boy's tone changed as he turned to walk away.

"Wait." Tallow pleaded.

The boy turned with a scowl on his face.

"I'm sorry. Since the marketplace fight I haven't had many friends. My name is Tallow." He stuck his hand out with a reassuring smile.

"Oh, I know all about you, and what you did that morning. My name is Kinsmor. The dog's name was 'Willy' and he'd gotten out of his pen. By the time I'd realized it, the boys were already chasing him down the street. I knew what they were going to do to him, but I was too afraid to stop them. There were so many times I wanted to thank you, but I was too ashamed." With that the boy stuck out his own hand.

The two boys grabbed each other's hands and shoulders and began a fast friendship.

Tallow was curious so he had to ask. "You said 'was'."

"What?"

"You said the dog's name 'was' Willy. What happened to him?"

Kinsmor looked down. "The wolves got him last winter."

"I'm sorry." Tallow's apology was genuine.

As the boys walked and talked through the halls surrounding the arena their attention was drawn to the mob of boys around the Clarion Board.

The boys looked at Tallow and made a path for him. Kinsmor stepped in front and snatched the paper from the board.

"It's Brutus." Kinsmor nodded. "He's the boy from the ma…"

"I know who he is." Tallow cut Kinsmor short.

Tallow scanned the paper as his eyes were drawn to "Brutus V Tallow."

"It seems that the fire is getting hotter."

With that he handed Kinsmor the paper and walked away.

Chapter 3

A Proving Conflict

The thud of whipping arrows sinking into burlap forms of men greeted Darius as he searched for a particular face. The high-pitched grunts of boys made him smile while they tried to mimic their heroes in combat.

The slap of wooden rods against a tight wrapped manikin brought Darius to the boy he was looking for.

He studied his movements and it piqued his curiosity even more. Every spin and kick the boy made had a purpose. Darius had seen this type of fighting in the Asian world, but this was a Roman citizen. His father was the town's blacksmith. Darius remembered what Rachael, the boy's mother, said and it made sense. 'He was born in the shade of a Tallow tree.' Those trees were plentiful in China.

"It's not you again." Tallow joked and rolled his eyes.

"I just came by to see how one of the 'dogs of Caesar' was doing." Darius mocked the morning greeter.

A grin crept across Tallow's face as he resumed a fighting stance.

"I'm glad that you're in good spirits, considering all that's happened to you."

Tallow shot a look back at Darius.

"Yes. I heard about that squabble you had with that oaf, Brutus. I wish I could've seen him holding his stones and squirming like a wounded snake. I would've..." Darius stopped when his eyes noticed the slumped shoulders and drooped head of his "champion". "Again? Boy, you have nothing to be ashamed of! Don't ever be ashamed of your skills or who gets in the way of them. Those skills will keep you alive.

"I'm not ashamed!" Tallow fired back at the soldier.

"I'll ignore the insubordination, but you've got to get through this guilt over beating someone. Guilt has no part of a Roman soldier's life. I'll do what I can to change the matches for now, but…"

"No. I don't need that." Tallow objected.

"Then what do you want? I'm still trying to figure you out, boy."

"Have you ever spent time with a blacksmith?" Tallow asked doubtfully.

Darius shook his head curiously.

"Is your sword made of steel or lead?" Tallow continued.

"It's made of steel." Darius said proudly.

"Have you ever seen lead in a fire? It turns to mush with very little heat. Brutus is not made of lead, so it will take a hotter fire to make him bend."

Darius' countenance changed when her realized what Tallow was driving at.

"I'm just tired of proving that I'm not made of lead either." Tallow said.

"I've seen less wisdom in warriors three times your age." Darius said thoughtfully. "I would shake your hand, but that wouldn't set well for either of us."

Much to Darius' surprise, Tallow winked at him as he turned to walk away. The boy just stood there grinning.

*****

The matches were set and all the opponents were glaring at one another. There wasn't really any venom behind their stares, but no one could let the other know that.

Tallow had to snicker with the others as Brutus approached the opposite line. He had the same, cocky air about him, but the physical lump sticking out of his loins shrouded it.

"Not this time." Brutus growled as he patted his groin.

With that the other kids broke into laughter.

"All right, you dogs of Caesar!" A familiar voice barked.

Tallow snuck a look at Darius and they both shared a smile.

"The time for 'mother' is gone. Forget her. Caesar is your mother, your father, your sister, and your brother. Your very life is Caesar's now. Your glory is Caesar's, so think of yourself as Caesar's."

The same voice seemed to get louder as it came closer to Tallow and Brutus.

"We will conduct a test of your skills with a gladius. It resembles the sword that you will use one day. We don't want you to kill each other before you die for Caesar." He gently gripped Brutus' shoulder, from which Brutus jerked away.

"Watch yourself, boy." The soldier murmured a caution to Brutus.

"Before the matches begin, you will practice three moves with each other. The upward block with the gladius," The man motioned a horizontal gladius above his head. "the slash block," The motion changed to the tip pointing up and sweeping to one side. "and the downward block." The man portrayed a chopping motion with the gladius.

"Never stop a gladius with anything but another weapon.

This is not only a good practice, it's easier than cleaning your blood off the weapon." A chuckle came from the garrison, but the kids were stone quiet.

"Now, you may begin."

The rattle of stone gladiuses filled the arena as the boys mimicked their leader. Kinsmor frantically blocked his opponent's blows with the example he had seen.

A yelling Brutus came at Tallow with his gladius, ready to split his head open. Tallow crouched with one leg sticking out as the breeze from the blade wisped his hair on the brute's way down.

"Want to try again?" Tallow quipped.

Before Brutus could get to his feet, the booming voice of the commander drew everyone's attention away.

"I said, 'Let me see your hand,' boy!" The commander barked.

It was Kinsmor the commander was speaking to. He had stopped a weapon with his hand and he had to be "taught a lesson".

Kinsmor's hand trembled as he slowly brought it out in front of him.

The commander raised the stone gladius above his head to chop the boy's hand off. He flicked his wrist to expose the flat side on the boy's hand. With one solid motion the stone came crushing down on Kinsmor's knuckles. He let out a scream that made even some of the seasoned soldiers grimace.

"Let this be a lesson to all of you. We tell you these things not just for your learning sake, but also for your life's sake. Carry on."

Tallow heard rushing footsteps behind and dropped to his knees.

A body flew over him like a sack of potatoes and flopped

against a post.

"I guess you did want to try again." Darius said as he smiled and lifted the boy to his feet.

"We're supposed to be practicing our defensive moves! Do you want to try it the right way now?" Tallow scolded.

"Well then, get ready to defend yourself."

Brutus came at Tallow with the same head-splitting swing as before. Tallow executed an upward block perfectly and swung the gladius at his opponent's rib cage. His blow was stopped and the point of Brutus' weapon came dangerously close. The boy slapped the tip downward while stepping aside.

Brutus shot him a look that said, *"I've been paying attention."*

"Haaalt!"

The dull clatter slowly stopped at the command.

"The matches will now begin. When your name is called, you will step to the center arena."

The center arena was nothing more than stones rising above the sand about five or six inches. It spanned a circle of fifteen feet in diameter. Inside, the circle was gouged with heel and knee marks from previous bouts. A man could step into the circle and see courage raise its head or fear cowering away.

"Tallow of Barsiebus and Brutus of Calpius come to the arena." Malcus announced.

The two stepped into the ring and faced each other. Then toward Malcus, they nodded their heads in protocol reverence. Malcus acknowledged their nod with a nod of his own, clapped his hands and said, "Begin."

Brutus fought the urge to rush in, considering the painful results of the last two times. His side was still reminding him of his last defeat.

Tallow's victories had ebbed his fears of the opponent before him. He was still guarded, but his mind was clear of any doubts that he had before.

Brutus was the first to break the standoff when he lunged with a side swiping motion. With a side step Tallow was quickly behind him. He knocked Brutus in the back of the head with the flat of the blade. Brutus turned and thrust his sword's tip at Tallow. A quick dodge and rap on the knuckles sent the big ox clutching his hand and stumbling away.

Tallow turned for a second to scan the crowd and sensed the evil coming at him. He quickly snapped the gladius above his head to catch the blow coming from behind. The crack of the stone and the lightness of the weapon in his hand sent a chill through his body. He quickly turned, grabbed the sword filled hand and, with a foot in his adversaries gut, fell back and flipped the wide-eyed Brutus behind him.

The crowd scattered as sword and body came rushing their way.

Tallow snapped up quickly and was approaching Brutus.

Brutus got up with his back to Tallow. He whirled around and threw sand in Tallow's face. Brutus then punched Tallow with a flurry of fists, all hitting their mark with solid contact. His blows didn't stop until Tallow tripped over the edge of the ring and was lost in the crowd. Brutus then turned smiling and walked back with his arms spread in an arrogant gesture.

Brutus stumbled forward after two flat hands hit his back. He turned in time to meet a foot with his face.

It was Tallow's turn to pummel this bully. He worked him over to the other side of the ring and knocked him to the ground. He grabbed a fistful of shirt and pulled the big oaf's head up. He then grabbed Brutus' gladius and pointed it inches from his chin. Brutus' eyes widened and the boys all gasped at the sight.

"I could run this to his spine." Tallow's thoughts rushed in. "You're not worth it." The words snuck out through Tallow's pursed lips. He flicked the weapon away and laid one final fist blow to the center of Brutus' face. Tallow walked off knowing his victory was secure.

Chapter 4

Malcus' Test

As time passed, Brutus and Tallow did not become friends, but they were no longer enemies. The knocks and bruises they gave each other were enough to convince them to choose another target.

The boyish games lost their appeal to Tallow as he worked on becoming a warrior. His skill with dual swords was improving as well as his quickness and agility. His opponents were not the only ones to notice his skills, but they paid the price for "noticing". Brutus' weapon of choice was a razor sharp axe. He was able to hack limbs off like wheat with a sickle.

*****

Malcus stood, with a rock in one hand and a stick in the other, looking intently at the tip of the stick. The tip was blunt and smooth now from the honing of the rock. Malcus rubbed his thumb across the tip to check his work. He was just eyeing the stick for straightness when Darius entered the room.

"What do you think?" Malcus asked, as he tossed the arrow at Darius.

"Is our next war going to be a peaceable one? Maybe we should blunt our spears as well, and use pillows for shields."

"I'll overlook your attempt at humor because of your ignorance. Your boy has become quick with those swords and I heard he left a ring of boys in a bloody mess with his fists. They say that no one can match his quickness----in close combat."

"What does that mean?" Darius didn't like where this was leading.

"Now, Darius don't let your skirt curl. It's just a safe little experiment I dreamed up." Malcus held up the blunt arrow.

"Dreamed is right. What if an iron tip slips in with these blunts and gets fired? It will be a nightmare."

"You've seen the boy's actions as well as I. Remember the story you told of the marketplace. This is the same principle, except its arrows instead of rocks."

Darius looked doubtfully at Malcus. "It might work, but Tallow has enemies that wouldn't think twice about 'accidentally' using an iron with the blunt ones."

"Oh, you mean Brutus." Malcus laughed. "He couldn't hit him if he were ten feet away. I'm asking you to trust me once again Darius. Will you?"

"Well, you were right about the matches. I guess I'll give this a shot."

*****

Tallow strolled down the arena hall as he'd done so many days and nights before. From out of the shadows emerged the man who'd started all this. Tallow didn't blame Darius much. He'd been a good friend through it all. This was like Darius to catch Tallow while no one was around, away from suspicious eyes. He said that he was protecting both of them.

Darius had a worried look on his face. (He always had a "worried" look when they met like this.)

Tallow now looked at Darius eye to eye. He no longer had to rub his neck after their conversations.

"Tallow. I don't have much time to talk, but I wanted to

prepare you for a little drill that Malcus has in store for you tomorrow."

"Whatever it is I'm sure we can handle it."

"This time, there will be no 'we'." Darius was apologetic as he told of Malcus' plan.

Chapter 5

Tallow's Answer

Tallow was enjoying himself while sparring with Kinsmor. His friend's hand had healed nicely from the crushing blow he's received in the early days. Kinsmor had trained himself to fight with the other hand, which gave him an edge. Tallow took great pleasure at the new challenge.

"Time." A bellowing voice came over the arena.

"We will continue this tomorrow. Sergeant."

"Yes, Sir."

"Take these men and dowse them with water. They all smell like sweaty sows." He said with a wink and a smile.

"Tallow. I need you to stay behind."

Tallow felt a lump in his throat. He knew what was coming.

As the young men thundered off, a few of the curious stayed behind. Kinsmor knew what was coming as well and he strained to swallow.

Malcus stepped forward and Tallow knelt in respect to his captain.

"Stand to your feet, son."

Tallow rose slowly and found it hard to look Malcus in the face.

"These drills are not just to sharpen your skills as a fighter, but also to test your weaknesses. Get your gladiuses and come to the arena."

Tallow walked a few steps and picked up the leather sheaths. His legs felt like timbers as he dragged himself to the arena.

"Pick up your chin. You're a soldier in Caesar's Army. All countries bow to Caesar and they will bow to you."

Malcus moved in to Tallow's face. "Listen, this is no different than the marketplace."

Tallow shot a look at Darius, to which he held his hands up in question.

"Don't blame Darius, I have eyes and ears that you cannot see." Malcus stated while walking. He quickly drew a blunt and shot at Tallow before anyone could realize.

In a flash two jagged pieces of wood dribbled at the soldier's feet, broken by Tallow's weapons. Everyone looked with astonishment as Malcus gave a reassuring smile.

"Archers! Take your positions." Malcus commanded as he wrapped Tallow's head with a blindfold. "I'll take it off when they're in place."

He spun Tallow around a few times just to be sure. When he's stopped, Tallow spread the weapons off to his sides. He slowly, ominously arched them in a cross motion.

Malcus jerked the blindfold off and scurried away, like a mouse from an angry cat.

He gave the command from a safe distance. "Shoot your mark!"

In a flurry of spins and twists, splintered arrows fell limply to the ground as Tallow bounded over the arena. When one wave ended he kicked a group of barrels, knocking the soldiers behind them into a watering trough.

The arrow shots got faster and closer together, but Tallow's gladiuses moved in a rage of blinding speed.

The dust settled and Tallow rose with his eyes locked onto one broken gladius. He jerked his head around and scanned the arena floor, retracing his steps in "battle".

He snapped up the arrow with the crumpled metal tip off the arena floor and he approached Malcus.

"Just an exercise?!" He spat as he threw the gladius with the arrow at Malcus' feet.

"Wait. Tallow!" Darius called him back.

"Everyone down here now!!" Malcus was furious.

The rumbling crowd assembled within minutes on the arena floor.

Malcus' tone had softened. "Who fired this arrow?"

The gang of young men stood looking at one another.

"It was me, Sir." The voice said, nudging his way through the crowd. "I didn't mean to, Sir, but I got caught up in the heat of battle."

Darius recognized the man as the same cocky whelp from the Clarion Board that day.

"The heat of battle?" Malcus said incredulously. He heard a few snickers from the crowd as the mood lightened. "Where were you positioned?"

"I was up on the south corner, Sir." He said a little proudly.

"About fifty paces, that was quite a shot."

The soldier just grinned back at him.

"Mark it off on the ground." Malcus said with his back to him.

The soldier walked and talked of all the targets he'd hit with a single blow. "…and I've been practicing with a pendulum. I've been…" His speech was cut short and he felt the arrow plunge deep through his bicep as he turned. He let out a raging grunt that everyone in the arena heard.

Malcus stood there with an empty bow. "Next time, check your weapon before you check your sights."

The soldier cut Malcus in half with his eyes, as he ran off clutching his arm.

"I told you he was ready." Malcus said as he slugged Darius and walked off.

Chapter 6

Barsiebus Sizes Brutus

The clang of red-hot metal greeted the Roman soldiers as they approached the Blacksmith's shop. The familiar smells blew their way with a gentle breeze in the air. All the faces were common to Barsiebus, except one.

"Good day, gentlemen. What can I do for you?" He said while eyeing the stranger.

"Well, Barsiebus, we have a small problem. We have checked the armory and can't find anything big enough for Brutus here." The soldier motioned him forward with a wave of his hand.

Brutus stepped forward and the sun was blocked by his shadow. Barsiebus looked at Brutus' feet and, with amazement, his eyes scanned to the top of Brutus' head.

"This is not a *small* problem. This will have to be done outside." Barsiebus said, grabbing a large notched piece of wood.

Brutus stood with his arms spread apart while the man set a bucket behind him. The man stretched to reach his shoulders, but soon gave up as the soldiers chuckled. He motioned for the taller of the two to come and measure.

"I need the length from the bend of the neck to the bend of the shoulder."

The soldier showed the mark on the stick with his thumb as Barsiebus scribbled on a parchment. He started to step down and Barsiebus pushed him back.

"You're not done yet. I need you to measure from the slope of the shoulder to the bottom of the trunk."

The soldier again mounted the bucket and walked the stick down the young man's back. "It's a full length plus this." His thumb again pinched the stick at his mark.

Barsiebus raised his eyebrows at the mark and questioned. "A full length plus this?"

The soldier nodded his head in agreement with a grin on his face.

"Wait here, please. I've got to check on some horse armor." The two soldiers laughed as the blacksmith turned. "You come with me." He motioned to Brutus.

Brutus threw a quick glance to his superiors and they nodded. He stooped as he walked behind the old man. The soldiers pointed and laughed. Brutus looked like a mammoth being led by a small monkey. When they reached the back of the shop, the man grabbed a spool of twine.

"Either bend over or kneel down. I need to measure that melon for a shell to keep your brains in."

Brutus dropped to one knee. The man still needed a bucket to reach his head.

"So, you're Barsiebus." He said with a cynical tone.

"Yes, I am. Have we met?"

"No, but I know your son, Tallow."

The very mention of his name made Barsiebus' heart lift and he could not contain his excitement. "How is he? Is he a good warrior? Is he fattening up good?"

Brutus stifled the man's enthusiasm with a raised hand. He then chose his words carefully. "I don't know how he would do in battle, but he split my face open a few times with his knuckles."

Brutus could see a twinkle in the old man's eyes. He would let this man have his dreams. After all, he barely knew him. Why bring him down with what he really thought?

"So, how is Tallow doing? Are you two friends?"

Brutus had to think quickly. "Sir, do you know how big the Roman army is? I barely know who bunks next to me, much less who I fought the previous day."

"Oh, I didn't realize how vast the Roman army had gotten." Barsiebus said, knowing he'd overstepped his boundaries.

"I've gotten all I need. You can go and play soldier now." The slight dig produced a glare from Brutus as he walked back to the others.

"I'm through with your boy." Barsiebus added an insult to Brutus, who was now thoroughly irritated. "You can expect the armor in two weeks."

*****

Darius peered over the wall at the familiar rider approaching the gate. He wasn't battle weary, but the horse's quick pace told of an urgent message. With a nod, Darius sent the order to "Open the gate." Chains clinked and wood groaned as two massive timber gates opened, welcoming the rider.

Malcus met Darius at the base of the wall and the two continued on to the messenger. The parched rider finished gulping and spraying himself with water as they approached.

"It's the Northern Army, Sir. Our men on the outskirts say they're planning something. The army hasn't raided any villages yet, but plenty of horses have been stolen in the past few weeks."

"How do you know it was them?" Malcus asked.

"One of the men on night patrol saw them take some horses. They put an arrow in him as he cross-bowed their leg. He'll be okay. The wound wasn't mortal."

"So their archers are getting sharper." Malcus thought out loud. "Darius, make sure your men all have shields and know how to use them."

"Yes, Sir." Darius walked away thinking. *"It looks like our proving ground will be to the north."*

That evening as the men were settling in, Darius addressed all of them.

"It seems as though some young whelps to the north have been stealing our cattle. They are taking horses to be precise. You may say, 'That's miles away from us, it doesn't affect us.' The Northern Army is not just stealing horses. They're preparing for war. Those are for their army. When I say our cattle, I mean they've been coming onto the lands of Rome. These are the same lands that Caesar would give you some day."

Darius went on rallying for Rome, but was careful not to work the men into a frenzy before "lights out".

The next morning, after the "dogs of Caesar" speech woke everyone, they were shuffled quickly to the armory to get weapons and field armor. One of Brutus' superiors dumped a bundle of armor in front of him and said. "Barsiebus came through for you sooner than we expected."

The trunk shell passed over Tallow's head causing him to remember his father doing the same thing years ago. He laughed at the memory of stumbling under the load. He could still remember his father's wink and smile.

"Tallow. Do you want to join the army?" Darius broke into Tallow's thoughts.

He shook his head as he smiled at his own embarrassment and started toward the door.

The whole garrison was bustling with excitement; they were ready for the battle for which they were trained. Some boarded wagons and chariots while others marched, but they had one goal--- the Northern Army.

Chapter 7

The Northern Battle

Darius watched as the Northern Army lined up for battle. Their faces were as fierce as young hyenas approaching their first kill. Their masses had grown since the Roman Army last squelched them. Darius thought this young crowd would be a challenge, but not a threat to his men.

He looked at his own line. The comparison didn't worry him. They could match strengths with anyone. What he worried about was the numbers. This army they faced, as inexperienced as they were, made up for it in size.

Darius could think of a few of his own men that would fight as five. Brutus could take out a line with just his bare strength, while Tallow could lop off heads and hands like butter. This day would prove his soldiers' worth.

The men poured out onto the field in tight formation while Darius barked out orders. "You men spread the ranks on the East end! We don't want them to out flank us. Make your mark and check your weapons. This time we want them to feel the sting."

Everyone looked at Grayboe and laughed. His face turned red as he messaged the old wound.

The Northern Army sent their horses and foot soldiers in an angry throng.

"Archers! Unleash the fury!" Darius yelled.

A great sea of white sticks arched over the sky, like cattle over a hilltop. Each arrow hit its mark, mowing down the thundering hoards.

The clash of the two armies could be heard for miles. The sound of metal clanging and scraping against shields was matched only by the grunts of men fighting and dying.

Tallow swiped across a soldier's neck with his blade, producing a shower of blood across his face. A duck and a back kick to the crotch of another assailant sent the man doubled over. His head fell to the ground with the hack of Tallow's blade. He heard a thud and a grunt behind him. Brutus pulled the pointed axe from the warrior's spinal column.

No words were spoken, but the two affirmed each other as "comrades" with a nod of the head.

The Northern Army retreated over a small hill and the Roman soldiers ran after them.

"Stand down men! Do not pursue them! Stand down!!" Darius barked.

The army fell back and the men shouted their victory until the hillside rumbled with their voices.

Malcus knew the lay of the land and sent three scouts discreetly over the hill. The scouts came back with news of archers in the rocks. The army was being led into an ambush.

"How are they protected?" Malcus' strategic mind was working.

"The archers are tucked into the rocks with one foot soldier each to protect them."

"Here's what we will do, but we must make haste." Malcus said as he spread a parchment map over a stump. "Let the men keep yelling, but pull the archers to meet me over there." He pointed just a few yards away.

"Their archers are all here." He showed the range of rocks surrounding the valley on the map. "We'll place our archers here and here, while the rest of the army keeps them busy." His fat fingers singled out two wooded areas on opposite sides of the map. "The plan is for our soldiers to keep them in the rocks long enough for our archers to get them."

Malcus briefly scanned the crowd surrounding him. He clapped his hands to get their attention. "Listen to me carefully. Our complete victory is all depending on our total silence."

"Both wooded areas," he pointed to the patches on the map, "are within bows range of the ambush sight. While Darius and his men are keeping them busy, our arrows will be mowing them down like Caesar's wheat fields. Leave your swords here and anything that might clang against trees."

The men dropped their weapons in a heap and Malcus barked out another order.

"Leave the horses. Their noise will let everyone know that we're coming." A few glares shot his way while others laughed as their friends dismounted.

They quietly crept off the hill they were on, through a valley and to the forest's edge.

A soldier spotted them, but his journey was cut short by an arrow through the neck. Grayboe slowly lowered his bow and then wrapped it around himself. It felt good to hit his mark again. His arm had healed nicely from the arrow piercing his bicep.

Malcus motioned the men close to him and in a low voice he gave his orders.

"Listen and do exactly what I tell you. I want two lines formed parallel with that rocky knoll. The first line will be fifteen cubits this side of the rocks and the second line will be twenty cubits."

He then paused. "Does everyone know what a cubit is?"

The men chuckled.

"The lieutenant has his men on the opposite side doing the same thing. When we see the fire shot in the sky, then we will attack. You know your mark so get ready."

*****

"I hope the men are ready soon," Tallow said with a little disgust in his voice. "I'm getting weary of chasing this rabbit back into his hole."

Brutus snickered. "Yeah, but the rabbit gets smaller every time he goes back." They both shared a laugh.

Tallow studied Brutus as they were laughing. This was the first time they'd enjoyed a laugh together. He could see that their days as adversaries were coming to an end, and their days as comrades were just beginning….but for one thing.

"Brutus." Brutus looked at him with raised eyebrows. "In the heat of things, I didn't get a chance to thank you for putting a spike in that man's back. I hope things have changed between us."

Brutus looked Tallow over. The stern expression on his face melted away when he detected softness in Tallow's voice.

"From that first day when you shot my grapes into my belly, I knew that you were a better fighter than me. I was so jealous and hated you for that. I was used to crushing my opponents without much effort. No one could match my strength. I was so proud that I couldn't be beaten, until you came along. It would've been easy to justify my hatred if you'd have been cocky or arrogant in any way."

"Someone like you." Tallow jested.

"Let me finish my own story." Brutus grinned. "You were

quite the opposite of everyone else. You were unassuming; never being the tyrant; always trying to be everyone's friend."

"I was really sickening." Tallow jibed.

"I thought so myself until I saw a little servant girl in the village trying to be friends with a mongrel. She would take scraps of food from the market to the little beast. All it did was snarl at her and wouldn't touch the food until after she left. I often asked her why she didn't leave it alone and find an animal that liked her. Do you know what she told me?"

Tallow just shrugged his shoulders.

"She said. 'Someone taught this little creature to hate people. I'll teach him to trust people.' I thought to myself. That dog was not unlike me. I had all this strength and I gladly used it on anyone despite how nice they were to me. The girl eventually won the dog over. He's big enough now to tear her in pieces, but he won't because he loves her. I'm still new at showing kindness, but will you take my hand as a friend?"

Brutus' hand swallowed Tallow's and they both shared an embrace.

"There's the sky fire." Tallow observed an arrow flaming through the sky.

"Get ready. That scrawny rabbit will be coming at us again." Brutus joked.

*****

"Launch your furry!" Malcus gave the command and almost simultaneously arrows came from both sides of the rocks.

Before the Northern Army could react, they were cut down with a shower of arrows. The archers fell first. The few that were left were captured and brought before Malcus.

"Who leads this rabble set before me now?" Malcus

demanded. "What? No volunteers. You were so brave on the field with swords and shields. Did someone cut out your tongues?"

"Our officers…are dead, Sir." A shaky voice from the line uttered.

Malcus went to where the voice was. The young man was still trembling over a puddle that he had created.

"Why are you still alive? You should've laid down your neck for your captain."

With that Malcus ran his sword all the way through the man's trunk. The man's face gasped in horror as his life slipped away. Malcus pulled his weapon from the quivering body and the crowd backed away.

"Tell your king that Rome will not tolerate trespass of any kind. Next time we will march against your kingdom." Then he muttered. "Set them free."

As the army scampered away, Malcus ordered the archers to fire just behind them. The arrows struck and the army rushed over the next hill. The men all broke into laughter at the sight.

"Let's go home." Malcus chuckled and turned his horse.

Chapter 8

The Quest Begins

Kinsmor noticed a faint light in the halls as he walked through the garrison. He approached the light and found his friend deep in thought of the day's events.

"I would've thought that you'd hit the sack early, considering how you fought today." His words fell dead in the air. "Tallow, what's weighing so heavy on your brow?" He was worried.

"I spoke with one of the warriors before he died." Tallow said, still deep in thought.

"He was begging for mercy, no doubt." Kinsmor joked.

"It was quite the contrary. He asked me if I 'knew the one he was going to meet'. He had such a look of peace on his face."

"The gods must've been good to him." Kinsmor reasoned.

"It wasn't *the gods*. He talked of a man named…Jesus?" Tallow questioned.

"Oh. Ciaphus had that man, Jesus, but he delivered him to Rome to kill, because the Jews didn't want to get their hands dirty." Kinsmor was a little irritated.

"He talked of being…forgiven." Tallow continued. "I asked him of whom did he need forgiveness? He said that he was forgiven by the Creator when he believed in Jesus as the Christ, the Messiah."

"Yes, I know of that Jew and all that he claimed. If you ask me, anyone that is affected by that man has been changed into a weakling."

Tallow slugged his friend and received a scowl.

"Some are weak before they even hear of the man." Tallow winked and grinned.

A sheepish grin spread across Kinsmor's face as he rubbed his shoulder.

"Remember, you're a Roman soldier. You have no lord but Caesar. You don't need that Jew's religion." Kinsmor said, trying to discourage his friend.

"You recite our leaders well, but how do you feel about forgiveness? My friend, everyone needs forgiveness at some point in his life." Tallow admitted as he walked off.

*****

The morning yawns were barked awake and the men fell in line at the arena. Drooped eyes from too much ale greeted Darius as he scanned the line with a knowing smile.

"Was the ale good last night, Brutus?!" Darius yelled in his ear.

"No, but she was!" Brutus yelled back and produced a dull chuckle from the men.

"With our last victory over the Northern Army, Caesar has given you a reprieve from your normal routine of the day. I didn't think you needed a reprieve, but judging from the look of your sad sagging faces, we wouldn't get any work out of you anyway." A few men laughed while the rest moaned. "Go back to your barracks and wait for your orders."

The men ambled back while Tallow caught Darius' attention. "Captain, could I have a word?" He seemed anxious.

"Yes." Darius motioned him aside. "What's on your mind?"

"Well, I heard a rumor that Rome was sending soldiers

throughout the empire to strengthen the weak boundaries. Is there any truth to that?"

"Maybe, why do you ask?" Darius was irritated that Tallow knew of Rome's plans.

"I'd like to be put on patrol in Jerusalem, if at all possible."

Darius was a little reluctant. "I'll see what I can do, but only the privileged few go there."

Tallow thanked him and started to walk away.

"Tallow." Darius stopped him. "Why Jerusalem?"

"Let's just say I have a lot of questions that can't be answered militarily."

"Are you considering 'conversion'?" Darius asked suspiciously.

"What is conversion?" Tallow questioned.

"Never mind. Your question answered mine." Darius smiled as he turned and walked away.

Chapter 9

The Conversation

Darius looked at the man that stood before him now. He was much different from the reserved boy that walked into his garrison years ago. He was no longer timid and shy, but could stand toe to toe with virtually anyone in the army, including some of the officers. The conversation he needed to have would be difficult, but it had to take place to ease his doubts.

"Tallow."

Tallow broke from his work and walked over.

"I spoke with Malcus and some of the senators. You will go to Jerusalem, but we're worried that you'll lose your focus."

Tallow studied Darius for a moment. "What do you mean?" He asked guardedly.

"Some of our finest warriors have lost some of their ferocity from their stay at Jerusalem. Some say it's because of that Jew, Jesus, preaching of love and mercy. I just don't want you to fall like the others." Darius sounded worried.

Tallow remembered Kinsmor's words. "I haven't met this…Jesus of whom you speak, and now he's dead so why worry about it?" Tallow said, knowing he still had questions that he dare not speak.

"Just remember where your allegiance lies. You're a Roman soldier. You are one of Caesar's finest. Mercy is for the weak. Pay no attention to Jesus' disciples; they'll only cloud your mind with doubts of your purpose."

"My allegiance should not be in question, most especially by you. Haven't Brutus and I been the first you call to lead the men into battle?" Tallow's voice was rising.

"Yes." Darius was remaining calm.

"When Caesar needed a special guard set around him for three days, was I not the first to volunteer?"

"Yes, you did." He tried to calm him.

Tallow's reaction to Darius was just the assurance that he needed to answer all of his questions.

"Rest assured my friend; this wasn't meant to be an inquisition. I just wanted to silence some skeptical senators." Darius gave Tallow a comforting smile.

Tallow's charade worked for now, he thought. He still had to guard what he said. Someone was always watching.

Chapter 10

The Melon Girl

When he arrived in Jerusalem, Tallow's orders were simple. Put down any rebels and keep the streets at peace.

This wasn't a hard task to do. How many "rebel" Jews were there in Jerusalem? To his knowledge, the streets weren't exactly teaming with rioters.

His thoughts drifted back to the words of the fallen soldier. *"Do you know Jesus, the one I go to meet?"*

The man spoke of such hope in the afterlife; surely he wouldn't be denied access to this "God Almighty" that he spoke of.

It made Tallow think of his own life. *What was his purpose? (Other than what Caesar dictated.) What did he want to achieve with his life?*

While he pondered these questions, his stomach was telling him of another "need"… food. He thought the market would have something small to offer.

The sounds coming from the market reminded him of his childhood. He almost expected to be hit in the mouth with a fish.

"Sugar dates! Your mouth will love them." A man rang out.

Dates sounded just right for now. When he approached the man, he lunged with a knee down, catching a melon inches above the ground.

"You're lucky he caught that or you'd be paying for it." The vendor barked.

"I'm paying for it anyway." The woman snapped back. "This is for breakfast." She then turned to Tallow. "Thank you sir. I appreciate your kindness."

"Kindness is something everyone should show, whether it is great or small."

"You sound like a man I once knew."

"Was this man good at showing kindness?" Tallow spoke gently.

"He showed more than kindness, he showed forgiveness." She said with a break in her calmness.

Tallow could guess whom she was speaking of, but he had to ask. "Was this man named Jesus?"

"Yes, he was, if you knew him, you must know of his death."

"I didn't know him, but I've spoken to those who did. I first heard of him from a dying soldier, even in his last breath he praised him. Everyone I've spoken to since has had nothing but good to say about him, except my superiors. When that dying soldier told me about Jesus, I wanted to meet him. When I'd heard of Jesus' death, I wanted to come to Jerusalem and find out more. That's what brought me here."

The woman was taken by Tallow's words. He was a Roman soldier who wanted to know about Jesus. She didn't know what to expect, but she was willing to take a chance at his kindness.

"Sir, I was a woman that Jesus rescued from death. I don't know if you're familiar with Jewish law, but my crime was one worthy of stoning. You see, I made my profession in the evening, awarding men's pleasures. The Scribes and Pharisees had never bothered me before Jesus came. My lover and I were taking our fill of loves, when the Pharisees burst in and grabbed me. They barely let me grab my clothes as they dragged me along. They cursed me and slapped me all the way to where Jesus was. They threw me before him and all I could do was cower at his feet. I didn't know him. I didn't know if he sided with the crowd screaming their hatred of me. I expected to feel the sting of rocks as I cringed there at the temple, but Jesus silenced the crowd that cried for my blood. I still couldn't look up from my shame as he raised me to my feet. He took my chin in his hand and said, 'Woman, where are your accusers?' I looked around us and no one was there, Even the Pharisees were too embarrassed to stay. 'No one, Lord.' I said. He looked me in the eyes and said, 'I don't condemn you. Go and sin no more.' I felt as if this man saw to my soul that day, but he forgave me anyway. I didn't go back to what I was and I finally feel…clean."

"You felt forgiveness just from looking into his eyes. What kind of spell did he cast on you?" Tallow was doubtful and genuinely concerned.

"It wasn't just his gaze, but his words. 'I don't condemn you.' He spoke with such authority and compassion. I couldn't help but listen and do what he said."

Her words of forgiveness struck Tallow's heart. When she spoke of Jesus seeing to her soul, it intrigued him more. *Was this man a god, or did he just have a way of controlling one's mind?* Tallow wanted to know more, but his questions were subdued by his position. Darius' words echoed back to him. "You're a Roman soldier. Pay no attention to Jesus' disciples."

Tallow knew of whom Darius spoke, but Jesus had certainly changed this woman. He felt a longing to experience what she had. Forgiveness was something a Roman soldier was not to give or receive, but it was something that he desperately needed.

He felt the need to speak to someone who had been with Jesus every day, but who would feel free enough to speak of such things to a man of his stature and position.

Chapter 11

Midnight Meeting

"*The marketplace is quiet today.*" Tallow's thoughts invaded his boredom. The thought rushed out at the sight of a beggar's fingers wrapped around a piece of fruit. When he turned and poked the fruit into his coat he met the soldier chest to chest and fell back a few steps.

"I won't say anything if you put it back." Tallow promised. "In fact, if he sees you, I'll tell him it fell and you were dusting it off."

"What? Are you talking to me?" The ragged man got louder.

"Unless the apple you took sprouted ears, I guess I am talking to you!" Tallow matched the man's voice. "Do you know the price you'll pay?" He shouted with the beggar's arm stretched out and his sword drawn.

"Stop. I'll pay for it."

Tallow's head shot in the direction of the voice and then to the cart owner.

"Money is money to me, as long as it's paid for." The owner shrugged.

With that gesture, everyone eased and the beggar ran away.

Tallow walked to the voice with his sword still drawn. "Do you make a habit of rescuing thieves in the marketplace?" He angrily scolded.

"I just rescue those who are about to lose a limb." The man said bluntly.

"What is your name?" Tallow's tone relaxed a bit.

"My name is Nicodemus. I'm a Pharisee."

"I knew that by your clothes. Why do you care about a man in rags, who probably has stolen from your coffers?"

"I didn't, before I met…"

"Don't tell me. Let me guess. Jesus. Right?" Tallow was still irritated.

"Yes. Did you know him?"

Tallow leaned forward, keeping his voice down. "No. I will speak more on these things, but not now."

"Are you asking me about Jesus?"

Tallow stifled him with a quick raised hand. "Meet me here at nightfall. I have some questions that no one has been able to answer."

"What a big surprise. He wants to meet me here at nightfall. That sounds familiar."

"What was that?"

"Nothing. I'll be here." He smiled as he walked away.

*****

The evening came and Tallow found an excuse to go out. He dressed in common clothes so as not to draw attention to himself. The general's words came back to him. *I have eyes in places that you know not.*

The streets were quiet except for a few beggars shuffling about. It looked like someone else had the same idea as he did. He recognized Nicodemus in spite of the tattered clothes and scraggly hair.

"So, my friend, you want to know about Jesus, but you don't want anyone to know that you asked. Is that it?"

"I may not be wearing the armor, but I'm still a soldier of Rome. I'll ask the questions. First of all, were you very close to the man? Did you know how his mind worked?"

Nicodemus stifled his questions with a raised hand. He didn't want this soldier to get ahead of his answers.

"I'd heard him teach in the synagogue and I knew there was something peculiar about this man."

"There were rumors about this possibly being the promised Messiah, but I dismissed them as being tales of wild imagination. His speech and demeanor drew me to him, because he took the position of authority in relation to heavenly things. I had to talk to this man one to one, so I arranged to meet him by night. I came to him in much the same way we're meeting now, but neither of us wore any disguises.

I started to talk about his teachings and he talked of man's need to be 'born again'. I'd never heard those words before, but he was patient and explained that it wasn't a physical birth that he spoke of. Then he went to the source of my problem.

For years I had studied the law, carried it out to the letter, and made sure that others did the same. I'd known the law and the prophets so well that no one could match me, before I met him. He meant no harm to anyone. He said that he came 'not to do away with the law, but to fulfill it'. He confronted my religious pride and asked, 'Art thou a master of Israel and know not these things?' He wanted me to see that God wants us to keep the law, but what He really wants is a deep, meaningful relationship with man. That is why Jesus came, to fulfill the law and to pay sin's penalty on the cross once and for all. Maybe you have the same problem as I do, pride."

Tallow was surprised and scowled at him, but kept listening.

"You've had years of people telling you how good you are, not only as a warrior, but as a person. When everyone says well and no one says ill, even the most humble of people can have a problem with pride. My own pride had tangled me up inside, but when I surrendered to God I found freedom. My friend, don't get caught in a prideful web of your own making."

"Since when are you, a Jew, judge over me?" Tallow snapped with venom in his voice. "I asked about Jesus, not about you!"

He stormed off and left the Pharisee in the street.

"What was it about Jesus that would change people's way of thinking? The harlot said that he saw to her soul. This Nicodemus said that he confronted him with his pride. Could this man be who they said he was? Could he be God in the flesh? And what did it mean to be 'born again'?" Tallow shook his head to clear his mind of the telling questions. That night he didn't get much sleep.

Chapter 12

The Assassin's Plot

Tallow rose from his bed, which didn't give him much comfort the night before. His questions and conscience fought his sleep all through the night. His whole body ached as he walked down the hallway. He wasn't ready to face anyone, much less one of his new superiors. He slumped onto the doorframe of his commander's post.

"You requested me?" Tallow moaned.

"Not really, but I got stuck with you anyway." The commander grunted.

Tallow didn't like his play on words and turned to leave.

"I'm still your superior; turn and face me! Stand at attention!"

Tallow turned to face the man and reluctantly straightened his body in attention.

The commander got right next to Tallow's ear and murmured. "I'm not half as impressed with you as Darius was, especially after that incident with the beggar."

Tallow shot his eyes at the commander.

"Yes. I too have eyes in the marketplace." He paused. "I have another assignment for you that is not much different from the one you're currently on. You will choose ten men that are battle ready, like yourself, to patrol the streets with."

"Is there a reason for the extra force, or did you just need them to baby sit me?" Tallow didn't hide his irritation.

"Don't flatter yourself. They've got better things to watch, I'm sure. The point is, make sure they're combat ready. Rumor has it that an assassin is either coming to us or is here already."

"Senator Potemus is supposed to examine our garrisons within the next few days, but I wouldn't put it past him to do a surprise inspection."

"The assassin would be insane to try something in the Great Hall." Tallow reasoned.

"That's why I want you and your men to patrol the streets. You know the route the Senator will take. Make sure the way is safe.

"Well, it is something out of the ordinary. I'm not sure about the men though, from what I've seen they're a bit 'green'." Tallow was noticeably troubled.

"According to your reputation, everyone is 'green', as you put it. This assignment is not so much for the Senator's protection, as it is to silence your skeptics. I, for one, don't believe half the things I've heard about you."

*****

Tallow's eyes were sharp tonight. The Senator had decided to inspect the troops at night to surprise everyone. Tallow and his men were ready at a moment's notice. The way was clear and the men knew their positions. Everything should run smoothly.

His commander came up with a quick step. "You'll have to choose the East passage around the temple. Someone turned a dung cart over, blocking the West." He said while shaking his head.

"Who cleans out stalls at nightfall, much less moves a dung cart at night?" Tallow's suspicions rose.

"A well paid pig farmer does. I'll need men to help move the cart." The commander wasn't really asking.

"You three go with the commander and keep your heads clear. Give me that!" Tallow snatched a pouch off the mouth of a tilted head enjoying the swallow.

"These men are yours now." Tallow gestured to the commander. "And I picked some of the best."

Tallow had an uneasy feeling as he approached the side of the Temple. He looked west and saw the commander and his men still grunting over the dung cart. The east path was dark and foreboding. He could see dim light at the corner of the Temple, but stone pillars on each side provided a perfect perch for a "would be" assassin.

"Is something amiss?" The worried, skinny, little senator asked.

"You did want to surprise the men, didn't you? This way is not what they'll be expecting. It will be fine, Sir." Tallow thought quickly.

"Yes. Good plan. I hope we won't find them sleeping." He laughed and went back to his place.

"Men. Tighten up around the Senator."

The circle moved in closer and the little man wiped a cloth over his forehead while he swallowed hard.

The darkness closed in as the mob crept down the path between the towering buildings. Each man's knuckles grew white on their swords as they quick-stepped around each pillar. The dark silence was broken by the wisp and thud of a spike in a soldier's back.

Blades flashed from everywhere as bodies and limbs were thrown to the ground. Tallow crossed his swords and sliced through his attacker's neck, leaving nothing but bare shoulders. The body fell before him and he leaped toward the Senator. A sword filled hand dropped to the ground while a grimacing young man ran off clenching a bloody nub.

The soldiers stood with their swords glimmering in the moonlight, their attackers had lost their vigor and were whimpering off. Tallow relaxed the grip on his swords. The now shaken Senator was wiping blood splatter from his face.

"I see why your commander chose you to lead this team. Your skill with the swords is outstanding. I owe you my life. Thank you."

The commander and his men heard the clash and had arrived with blades drawn.

"You're a little late commander, but your man already took care of the problem." The senator was a little irritated.

"We came as soon as we heard the trouble." The commander tried to excuse himself.

"While you and your men were playing in the dung heap, this man was opening my assassin's throat with his swords."

"How many men are left?" The commander tried to change the focus.

"We lost one, Sir, and one man has a deep gash in his right leg. We may need to put fire to it."

"Well, then do you need some men to hold him down while it's done?"

"Now you ask?" The senator chided in the background.

Tallow smirked, but ignored the senator. "Possibly. He's a horse of a fellow with a stubborn streak."

"That would be 'Bull'," The commander quipped. "You'd better take all of the men. I'll meet you back at the barracks."

The men followed Tallow and they braced themselves for a battle without weapons. When they reached Bull, they found him curled up beside a pouch of wine, like a lamb beside its mother. The attendant with him just shrugged his shoulders in disbelief.

*****

The commander was all smiles as Tallow approached his quarters.

"I've been hearing from the men about your actions the other night. The senator was not the only one impressed by your skills. The men said that you 'crossed' a man's head off. What is that?"

Tallow flashed his blades out in a crossing motion, to startle the commander, and then finished it the way he did that night. (Minus the head.)

"Well, you can rest assured that the senator will not keep his mouth shut about this. The Senate will be buzzing about it within the week. You've had a busy week. Have the gods been good to you? I hope you've gotten a good rest." The commander sounded gracious.

"Somewhat. My nights have been less tense, with the assassination squelched. That young buck will be pawing his food like a horse from now on.

They both enjoyed a laugh over that.

"I'm glad that you still have your sense of humor about these things. I'm going to give you and your men a break with 'light' guard duty for a while.

"How light of duty is it?"

"It's patrolling around the Jewish temple in daylight. I don't think there'll be any riots around there. Do you?"

"Not likely." Tallow stated while walking and then turned back. "Thank you, Sir."

"Think nothing of it. You've earned it." The commander's response was genuine.

Chapter 13

The Trouble Maker

Tallow's day was calm, but his men were getting restless. This group of men were getting better with their weapons, but they weren't what he was used to. They didn't have anything in common but fighting, and that only went so far.

His ears perked up with the sound of shouting down the street. His eyes cut across the street to Bull, as they both shook their heads and flashed their swords.

A boy came running with news of a riot.

"Sir, I think all Jerusalem is in the street. They're beating a man to death!"

"Who is the man?" Tallow demanded.

"Some man that they called a her…uh…tic."

The other soldiers came rushing up at the commotion.

Tallow quickly barked out orders. "Get as many men as you can down to the Jewish Temple." He signaled to one soldier. "Bull, you and the rest come with me."

The crowd parted as they saw the gleam of soldiers' blades in the sunlight.

A man covered in dust, was struggling at the crowd's feet. His hands were calloused and his face was cut from their actions. It was the man that they called Paul. He raise himself to his knees and a man came out of the crowd.

"Stay down! Heretic!" The disgusted scribe placed a foot in

Paul's ribcage.

The scribe was knocked into a column and he felt a thin line of cold steel on his neck.

"Do you want another mouth to taste my blade with?" Tallow asked. His men quickly surrounded him, with their swords drawn, facing the crowd.

Tallow left the scribe and lifted Paul to his feet.

"What's your name?" Tallow asked. "What did you do, that the whole city is in an uproar against you? Do you speak Greek?"

Paul was silent.

Voices from the crowd leveled their accusations. "He teaches heresy." "He brings Gentiles into the Temple." "He's a heretic."

Tallow thought. *"The crowd gets uglier, the longer we stay."*

"You men carry this man upstairs and out of this crowd." The soldiers around him stood firm, with their swords still out protecting their captain and Paul. Six men came and hoisted Paul onto their backs as the crowd drew in closer.

"Back off!" Bull shouted as he swiped the air, nearly taking off a man's hand.

The crowd separated and made a path leading up to the stairs.

The mob's voices were getting louder.

"Up the stairs." Bull demanded. "Get us out of this crowd."

Paul motioned to Tallow from atop of the soldiers.

When Tallow drew near Paul asked. "Do you speak Greek? I would like to talk to you."

"I just figured out who you are. This is not your first uproar. You're that Egyptian that led four thousand men out into the wilderness to their deaths." Tallow made his accusation.

"I am a Jew of Tarsus, a city of Cili'cia. I am no barbarian from any mean city. Please, let me speak to the people."

"I'll give you license, but guard your tongue," Tallow warned "or I will cut it out myself."

Paul held up his hand and the throng of angry shouts turned to subdued murmurs. The people calmed and Tallow and his men relaxed as well. When the silence spread Paul began.

Tallow and his men heard all of Paul's speech, from his credentials as a Pharisee to his conversion on the road to Damascus. *"This was Saul of Tarsus."* Tallow thought. *"No wonder there was such venom in their voices. They view him as a traitor."*

When Paul told of God sending him to the Gentiles, the audience burst out again with, "Away with him. He's not even fit to live!"

"Take him to the hall and tie him to the scourging post. If he won't tell us what this is all about, maybe the scourge will." Tallow wanted answers and this stubborn Jew wasn't going to stonewall him for long.

The dungeon door creaked open and gonged shut in the distance as Paul's companions squeaked and scurried back to their hiding place. He could see through the eye that wasn't swollen shut, dimly lit Roman soldiers marching heavily toward the post he now rested on.

The centurion's key broke open the locks around Paul's wrists and he asked, "Are you ready for your examination?"

The soldiers laughed at his joke.

The soldiers bound his hands with leather thongs while Paul asked. "Are you carrying out the letter of the law? Are you scourging a Roman citizen who hasn't even been condemned?"

All three were taken back by Paul's words.

"You're a Roman?" The centurion asked.

Paul nodded, enjoying the terrified looks on their faces.

One soldier finished tying Paul and rushed off, with the other two right behind him.

*****

Tallow's eyes caught the centurion as he entered the crowded palace hall. He nodded Tallow away from the crowd.

"Sir, my men and I have done all that we care to do with this man." The soldier had a foreboding tone about him.

"What do you mean, 'all that you care to do'?"

"Tread lightly with this one. He's a Roman citizen."

"Who told you that he was Roman?"

"He did, just as we were binding him to the flogging post." The soldier repeated the conversation.

"Come with me, gentlemen. Let's see this 'Roman citizen'." Tallow walked with the soldiers and contemplated his conversation with Paul.

"My men tell me that you're a Roman. Is this true?"

"Yea it is." Paul answered.

"Why didn't you say this before?" Tallow scolded.

"No one asked me."

Tallow didn't hide his frustration. "How much did you pay for this freedom?"

"I was born a free Roman citizen." Paul stated.

Tallow saw an opportunity. "Leave me alone with this man. I will examine him personally."

"Watch yourself." The centurion cautioned as he walked out.

Chapter 14

The Examination

Tallow didn't quite know what to expect from this man named "Paul". He had heard so much about him, but thought some of it only rumors as far as he could tell. His frame was well proportioned and his hands were calloused from his trade as a tentmaker. This wasn't what Tallow expected from one trying to "turn Jerusalem upside down," as the scribes put it.

He took the man's hands and removed the leather thongs.

"Before I turn you back over to the priests, I have some questions of my own."

"I'm sure that you do. I'll be glad to answer what I can."

"I'd like to know what you did, other than being a 'traitor', to raise the whole city against you."

"I brought Gentile believers into the synagogue."

Paul noticed the incredulous look on Tallow's face.

"They also hate me because I believe in the Messiah whom they rejected. I was once persecuting the followers of Christ in much the same way as the Jews do me now. I was on my way to Damascus with letters from the high priest. I wanted to kill the disciples of this 'Christ', and chain up anyone who believed the same way."

"Why? Did you ever meet the man?" Tallow still wanted to know about him.

"I was getting to that point. I never met him face to face."

"Just outside of Damascus a bright light shown from the heavens that knocked me from my horse and blinded me. Jesus called my name and asked me why I persecuted him so. I had a lot of arguments for his disciples, but at that moment their words were haunting to me. I was much like you are, well skilled in the Jewish religion, revered by the leaders, and able to defend this religion to a point. It is amazing how a voice and a blinding light can strip away the arguments in an instant.

My friend, you haven't had a blinding light experience yet. I pray that you won't let it come to that. You may have had people tell you all your life how good of a warrior you are. That might be good, if all you had was this life to worry about. The one true God has sent his Son so that we might have eternal life. He can give you the forgiveness and peace that your heart has longed for."

Tallow's pride wanted to strike this man in the face, but his heart submitted to the hope of true forgiveness.

"Why should I place my trust in this weak Jew's religion?" He asked halfheartedly.

"This is not a 'Jews' religion, as you put it. As I stated before, Jesus was the promised Messiah, the King of the Jews. His kingdom, however, was not of this world. He spoke to his disciples of a kingdom not built with hands. This is a kingdom that starts in your heart.

You see, the Jews rejected Jesus as their Messiah, and are still rejecting him. That's why my plea to accept God's plan of forgiveness is to both Jews and Gentiles. When Jesus was crucified, the veil to the Holy of Holies in the Jewish Temple was ripped by God himself from top to bottom. This shows to all who believe that through Jesus, they now have access to the Holy of

Holies. We can *all* have a relationship with God through Jesus, the Christ."

Paul noticed the well of tears growing in Tallow's eyes. "Forgiveness is yours, my friend, if you just ask."

"I have no king but Caesar!" Tallow shouted as he walked away. "Slap this man in irons!" He barked to the guard as he stormed off.

Tallow had to get away from there. The crust of pride around his heart was crumbling as Paul spoke of forgiveness. All of the speeches about being part of Caesar's army had swelled his ego farther than he had realized, or even wanted. Tallow knew that if he did pledge his allegiance to this 'Christ', it would be a pledge of his life. He wasn't ready for that.

Chapter 15

The Senate's Request

Tallow arrived at his commander's request, and recognized another face that he hadn't expected. Several others from the senate were all smiles as he entered the room. He didn't know what to expect, but he knew that he was summoned. *"Maybe they found my 'secret'."* A thought rushed from the back of his mind.

His worries were eased when Senator Potemus catapulted from his chair to greet Tallow. He jerked Tallow's hand up and down like he was cracking a whip.

"Tallow, old friend. It's so wonderful to see you again. How are the gods treating you?"

Tallow was taken back. "I don't know about the gods, but my commander has been tolerable."

They all shared a chuckle at the commander's expense.

The laughter was cut short by the commander. "There is a reason why we called you here. Senator?"

The Senator was irritated at the interruption, but excitedly addressed Tallow.

"Tallow, everyone here knows or has heard of how well you handle yourself on the battlefield, and your reputation with the men is unparalleled. That same reputation has reached the ears of Caesar. That's why we want to show your skills to the world…in the arena."

Tallow scanned the room and found nothing but hopeful

faces, like school boys wanting him to be on their team. Tallow's thoughts took him from the conversation.

"This would be a chance to get away from Christians. They wouldn't be anywhere near the games as spectators or players." He still remembered Paul's words of 'pride' and 'forgiveness'. *Paul was right about Tallow, and Tallow knew it."* His pride was still clinging to him.

"Tallow." A voice broke into his thoughts. His face flushed red as he snapped to attention and the daze left.

"You will be our champion, won't you?" His commander wasn't really asking.

"I will be willing to take this challenge on one condition."

"Let's hear the request." A skeptical senator sneered.

"I have served Caesar all my life. I have sacrificed my friends and my family to bring Caesar honor. My mother died of typhus while I was at war for Caesar." The venom was rising in Tallow's tone. "I think that I've earned the right to tell my father that his son is going on a suicide mission."

"What do you mean by 'suicide' mission?" Senator Potemus was surprised at Tallow's accusation.

"I'm no stranger to the gladiator games. It may start out as a man to man competition, but that won't be enough. It will soon turn into one against two or one against five, but even that won't be enough. They'll toss a hungry animal or two in the arena that is just as thirsty for blood as these senators." Tallow pointed his calloused finger at all the soft skinned, linen draped figures in the room, who were now scowling.

"Do you know who you are speaking to?" The skeptical senator snapped.

"Tell me that what I'm saying is not true." Tallow spat and an awkward silence fell over the room.

"I think we can agree, gentlemen," Senator Potemus spoke softly, "that this warrior needs a reprieve. One month should rejuvenate you. Should it not?" He nodded at Tallow.

Tallow reluctantly nodded back.

Senator Potemus stayed behind as the rest left the room, all glaring at Tallow.

The Senator approached Tallow cautiously. "What has given you this anger, my friend?"

Tallow waived off the senator. "It's not you, it's something else."

"Would you care to elaborate on that?" He acted genuinely concerned.

"No. I just wish my reputation wasn't so large."

"Your stay in Jerusalem hasn't 'changed' you has it?" Potemus was worried. "We did give you that freedom through our reservations."

"No, Sir. The last thing that I want to see right now is a Christian."

"I know. The 'love' and 'forgiveness' rubbish is creeping into our empire in subtle ways." Potemus noticed Tallow shaking his head and looking down in deep thought.

"Go home. Your father is calling you." He patted Tallow's shoulder as he left.

Tallow's thoughts troubled him. *"This was more than his father had hoped for, but he feared it was more than his father could take as well."*

Chapter 16

The Boy Returns

Barsiebus was sweeping molten spatter from around the caldron as he noticed a stocky man coming in on horseback. The horse trotted with the rider bouncing in the saddle. A gleam filled his eyes as he recognized his son. Tallow leapt from the saddle and gave his father a long hard embrace.

"My boy! My boy!" Barsiebus wailed. "My eyes are washed with joyful tears. It's good to see you again. What brings you back home to me? Have you earned a reprieve from your battles? What about that 'Brutus' fellow? Have you clocked him yet? Oh, I'm sorry. I'm rambling on and not giving you a chance to catch your breath. Come in and relax while I cook up some mutton for us to gorge on later. I see they haven't let you starve." He laughed and slapped Tallow's belly.

*****

As the evening sun was passing the horizon and Tallow's weary eyes were being lulled by the flickering fire, his father stood behind him contemplating his next move.

It had been a long time and he didn't know how much Rome had changed his son. Would he accept his father's news of conversion? There was only one way of finding out.

"Son." He spoke calmly, not wanting to disturb him too abruptly.

It didn't work. Tallow spooked from the lull he was in.

"I'm sorry. I needed to speak with you."

Tallow sat up straight. "That's part of why I'm back here. I have something of a serious nature to speak to you about. You first."

"I don't know how much contact you've had with Christians, but I understand Rome frowns upon them."

"Why are you worried about that?" There was a slight pause and then the realization hit Tallow with a shock. "Don't tell me that you're a follower of this 'Christ' they speak of. Father! Who has bewitched you into this way of thinking?" Tallow was visibly upset.

Although his fears were being realized, Barsiebus spoke calmly to his son.

"Let me explain as best as I can, before you act like I smashed your toe. When your mother passed, I got extremely bitter at life. I questioned what I had done to anger the gods. Why did my wife have to suffer so much?"

"I'm sorry I wasn't here for you." Tallow's compassion was stronger than his disappointment.

"A fisherman that I had made a helm for years ago stopped by. He said that he didn't fish anymore with nets and bait, but he drew men in. His name was Peter. He said that now his mission in life was to draw all men to Christ.

I told him about your mother and how she had suffered. He said, 'We can justify when the guilty suffer, but we can't understand why it touches the innocent as well.' He could see that I was suffering with her loss, and said that is why Jesus came. Jesus is touched with the feelings of our infirmities. He wants a relationship with us not only in this life, but in the one to come. Son, I don't know how to explain it, but I trusted in this 'Christ' he spoke of and since then I've found what I was searching for----peace. My life and my nights have been more at ease since then.

I'm sure you've made quite a reputation in the Roman army, and I'm very proud of you for that. Don't let that reputation cloud your judgment of what is good and right. Do you remember the dog in the marketplace? That is what is good and right, and it is what got you into all this in the first place. You were the defender of good."

Tallow remembered the helpless mongrel. He remembered his feelings back then. His father's words made what he was about to tell him that much more difficult.

He knew that he wouldn't be "defending" anything good or right in this bloody sport that Caesar obligated him to. There was nothing noble about him that his superiors wanted in the arena. He was good at killing another man; that's all they wanted.

"Father, this would be so much if you hadn't become one of *his* followers."

"I'm still your father and I still love you. What is so hard to tell me?"

"You were right. They did want me to take a reprieve, but I view it as a farewell. Caesar thinks that I'm such a good soldier that he wants me to try my skills in the arena. When I go back I will be a….gladiator."

They both said the word in unison. The silence captivated them both briefly. Barsiebus' eyes filled as he embraced his son.

"Father, don't worry about me. I've survived this long with hardly a scratch."

"Son, I know that you'll survive any opponent thrown at you, but think about this. When you consider the attitude that Rome has toward Christians, what makes you think that they are beyond throwing them into the arena?"

The realization of his father's words was all over his face. This would be a new twist even for Caesar, and Tallow would be in the middle of it.

"I'm sure it won't come to that father. I won't be the only gladiator that they have. I do have friends that are there as well."

"Don't tell me that 'Brutus' fellow is going to be with you."

"Yes."

"Is he with you or against you?"

"Those bridges were all crossed and burned years ago."

"Son, I know that this news of my conversion didn't set well with you. I just pray that God will give you peace. My nights of torment are over since I took the risen Christ as my Savior."

"That's all good for you, father, but *I will* decide whether I need this 'Christ' or not."

"Oh, you need Him, but your pride won't let you admit it. I'll pray for you, son." With that he left him alone and retired for the evening.

Chapter 17

The Road Back

Tallow's ride back was a welcomed journey. He enjoyed his father's company, but his new "faith" was almost unbearable. When his father's new friends came around, it was all Tallow could do to refrain from knocking his own head against a tree.

One thing that Tallow couldn't deny was the peace that he saw in his father's eyes. There was something there that he had not seen in him before. His compassion was greater than he'd seen in anyone, which wasn't saying much, considering his position.

"His position," Tallow thought. *"A man of his 'position' shouldn't be asked to take a 'position' like this."*

"What if I didn't go back to Rome?" Tallow's thoughts continued. *"What if I just gave it all up and became a blacksmith in some remote village, like my father? I would be hunted down like an animal for that traitorous act. I would be looking over my shoulder for the rest of my days and not know who to trust with my little 'secret'.* No. He needed to go back and fall in line with the others. At least that way he could see his enemy coming at him.

His thoughts drifted to the others, namely Brutus. He hadn't spoken to him since their conversation on the battlefield. He wondered if Brutus was still new at, how did he put it, "showing kindness."

Tallow's horse approached the hitching post and his eyes fell on a familiar face. The hair was still curly, but snow white, and he had a slight stoop in his stance. Tallow found comfort in his friend's face that had been there since the day they first met. He quickly dismounted and opened his arms.

"Well, Darius my old friend, how is one of the 'dogs of Caesar' doing?"

"I'm still barking and biting with the best of them!"

They both enjoyed a good long embrace.

"I'd heard that you might be coming back today. I understand that you ruffled some feathers before you left."

"They hit me with this stuff at the wrong time. I was upset about something else."

"I heard that you called the senators 'bloodthirsty beasts'."

Tallow's head snapped back. "Don't always believe what you hear."

"It's good to see that you've overcome your shyness, but that's taking it a bit far. Is it not?" Darius' slug was stronger than Tallow anticipated.

"Darius, I will start training as a gladiator soon."

"Yes. I've heard of that raw deal. I tried to get them to let me use you in training our warriors and I could also use a strong command in the field, but they are a determined bunch."

"So, I guess asking about the matches is out of the question."

"They've been rather tight-lipped, especially to me. I've heard that the Ethiopians are coming, but other than that, I'm clueless."

"What about the Senate? What is their general attitude?"

"They're very much anticipating your return. Some want their champion in the ring as soon as possible; others want you to die in the ring." Darius grimaced at the truth.

"Carnage seems to always impress the crowds." Tallow muttered as he walked away.

"I heard that." Darius grinned.

"So did the Senate and that's why I'm here."

Chapter 18

Tallow's Comrade in Arms

Tallow approached Brutus with caution. He always approached him with caution, but this time he had a sword in his hand trying to reach the calf of his leg with it.

"Give me that before you cut your leg off." Tallow commanded with a smile.

"I got a hunk of briar in it, I suppose, hunting rabbits a few days ago. It didn't bother me until today." Brutus apologized.

"Let's do this right. Step behind this wall." A familiar face passed by. "Kinsmor."

"Don't call the whole brigade in here!" Brutus panicked.

"I don't want your other leg to remove my head, you big ox. You should've let someone look at it sooner. Now I'll have to dig for it. Clamp your ivories down on this." He stuffed a thick piece of wood in his mouth.

Tallow sat with his weight balanced on Brutus' haunches while Kinsmor wrapped his body around the other leg. Several others, seeing the big man down, took great pleasure in holding onto any free limb sticking out.

Brutus' body tensed up as Tallow dug deeper. " 'Bout got it." Tallow stated.

Brutus let out a grunt and expelled gas.

"Let's hope the rabbit doesn't come out next." Tallow joked as the men laughed.

"I got it!" He shouted. "Give this man a drink and dress that leg."

The mob that held Brutus loosened their grip and patted his head as they left. His scowl only brought grinning faces from the same men, knowing that he couldn't do much. Kinsmor went to work on the wound, which wasn't easy, as the big man thrashed around.

"So, are you still as good with that axe as you were?"

Brutus launched the axe across the street, burying it in a crosscut piece of wood. Horses, spooked by the blade crossing their path, reared back and bolted down the street.

"Better." Brutus laughed. The ale was already taking affect.

"Good. I think I want you with me through these games."

Brutus was already nodding his head in agreement. Tallow patted him on the shoulder and started to walk off.

"Tallow."

Brutus extended his hand and Tallow grabbed it and hoisted his friend to his feet.

"I heard about your run-in with the senators."

"Who hasn't by now?" Kinsmor touted.

"I wanted to tell you that you aren't the only one who is, how did Malcus put it, a 'begrudging ally' of these games."

"That little servant girl really did change you, didn't she?"

"It was more than just the servant girl."

"Don't tell me that you're one too." Tallow's thoughts invaded.

He got right next to Brutus' ear. "If you are a 'Christian' your secret is safe with me, but you won't last long out there." The look that passed over Brutus' face confirmed his suspicions.

Tallow walked away as Kinsmor drilled Brutus with, "What did he say to you?"

Tallow was disappointed with the revelation of Brutus' conversion. He thought at least Brutus would be with him, not just in the arena.

"What was it about these 'Christians' that changed everyone he came in contact with? Maybe the religious leaders were right. They're turning the world upside down. His father's words came back to him. 'What if they put Christians in the arena?" This thought invaded most of Tallow's restless night.

Chapter 19

The Games Begin

Tallow's eyes popped open as the sun winked through a crack in the shaded window. He'd already missed the "dogs of Caesar" morning rouse. The distant clatter of weapons told him the arena was full of anxious young lads. He resisted the urge to join them. Instead, his stomach was drawing him in a different direction.

Kinsmor was the first to greet him as he turned toward the food court. He always had information that he knew you'd want to hear. (even if you didn't.) He was busting to tell Tallow, so he rolled hi s eyes and listened.

"You won't believe the beasts they've got for you to fight."

"I'm sure that you'll tell me." Tallow was annoyed.

"They've gotten the slaves of Germania. I heard that they drink the blood of their dead."

"You little rat hole, I haven't had breakfast yet!" Tallow scolded and pushed his friend.

"Good. The bakers have fresh bread for us this morning. It's really quite tasty."

*****

Not much conversation was exchanged around the breakfast table. Tallow wasn't the only one listening to his stomach. He and Brutus ate with such ferocity that the others stood about ten feet away in astonishment. (And maybe a little fear.) Brutus had a little fun by bursting out with a growl and faking a step toward them. He and Tallow laughed while everyone stumbled over themselves.

*****

The Clarion board boasted of the matches with the slaves of Germania. Tallow pushed through the crowd to see the notice of the event.

"Just three days, and we haven't seen the beasts. How are we supposed to prepare for them?" Tallow was incredulous.

"You will be in the arena first. Remember. They will be coming at you and they will be chained." A familiar voice reassured Tallow.

His head turned and his eyes locked onto his friend's face while his frown turned into a gentle smile.

"I know you don't think I need training, but I could really use a friend for the next couple of days. If you have the time, your trained eyes could be of use to me."

"It would be my honor to train you." Darius took a solemn tone. "I'm not as in charge as you may think. I've got time to spare." He crouched in a fighting stance as the two slugged each other and then shared a shoulder hug.

*****

The day of the matches had arrived and the men in the arena were tight with adrenaline coursing through their veins. Some were spinning their swords in their hands while others wielded spike iron balls on stick chains above their heads.

The gates of the arena burst open and the iron balls gouged into their opponents' cheeks, snapping their heads and throwing them to the ground. They poured into the arena like ants from their nest, moving along the walls and back into the battle.

Men used the chains between them to trip and strangle their opponents.

One young buck hacked his "partner's" hand off to free himself from the dead weight. He came at Tallow from behind, not seeing Brutus' javelin which pierced through his shoulder and stuck him to the ground. Tallow and the warrior's eyes locked onto a sword at his side.

"Don't do it! Let Caesar decide!" Tallow pleaded.

He defiantly snatched the sword up and swung. Tallow slapped it away and crushed his neck with a heavy Roman boot.

The fighting stopped and the dust settled on the Romans. Tallow stood angrily shaking his head at the young fool's effort. His eyes scanned the arena now patched with blood and carcasses. Men were wiping sweat and the refuse of battle from their faces while being attended by their subordinates. The few "visitors" left were allowed out of the arena, carrying their limping friends with them.

The Romans in the arena and the stands let out a tumultuous roar.

There was a time when Tallow would've raised his sword and cheered along with them, but now his eyes were fixed on the young man's body now quivering at his feet. His life was rapidly ebbing away as he raised his hand and pointed to the sky. A serene smile drew across his face as Tallow jerked his head to where the man was pointing. The sky was empty, but he knew what was there. He'd heard of the martyr Stephen's death, and his declaration as he died. *I can see my Savior standing at my Father's right hand.*

Tallow looked back as the young man's hand dropped and his body went limp.

A squire nudged Tallow with a cup of water which he gladly gulped down.

Tallow's thoughts raced as the rest of the men ambled to the arena exits.

"So this was the way it was going to be. Such savagery rewarded with so little effort. Even in war the enemy could run back to their homeland, but here everyone was at Caesar's mercy, including him. This brutal carnage was now his life, like it or not. He was ready to be a gladiator physically, but his heart was still battling over the soldier's dying words years ago. "Do you know the one I go to meet?"

"We'd better catch up with the rest before we become bait for the lions." Kinsmor jested as the lions roared in the background.

They both jogged to an exit and slapped the iron, gate shut behind them.

A lion's bursting roar and rattle of the gate made them both jump. Then they laughed at each other's embarrassment.

*****

Tallow's skills in the arena were unmatched by men. His somewhat prophetic words were realized when Caesar decided to test his skills against the hyenas of Africa in the gladiator games.

Tallow's arm was in an unfortunate hyena's jaws as his sword was run through the beast's pulsing heart. He fell limp at Tallow's feet while another lunged with gaping teeth at him. He darted aside, allowing the animal to sink into the belly of his "would-be" attacker. A grunted scream filled the air as the man fell backward with the beast jerking and shredding his belly apart.

Tallow had accepted that this was his life, but used every

opportunity to show mercy that he could. His sword play was not as aggressive and his kills were more of surprise than premeditation.

He still had questions about Jesus, but was careful who he asked and when he met them, now that the games were at a high point.

Chapter 20

Tallow's Surrender and Stand

Tallow's charade had fooled most of his associates, but a few watchful eyes of the Senate (those he called "bloodthirsty beasts") were looking for any excuse to ambush him. He was one of the primary subjects discussed behind closed doors.

"You can think what you will, but I think after his stay in Jerusalem, your hero has turned into nothing more than a lamb in wolf's skin."

"Has anyone been watching the games? The people want blood, and they want this 'Tallow' fellow to give it to them."

"Is that so?" Senator Potemus chimed. "I hear something quite the contrary. Some in the audience had to rush out and lose their breakfast. The venders say that they couldn't sell anything. The sight of a hyena splattering a man's belly on the arena walls would make lunch less appealing. Wouldn't you say, gentlemen?"

The senators raged on carelessly as a pair of ears just below the window basked in what was being said. A smirk crept across Tallow's face as he scoffed and walked away.

*****

Tallow gazed into the moonlit skies and laughed once more at Senator Potemus' pointed remarks.

"Sir."

He turned to the voice off in the distance.

"Yes, madam." His tone was gracious.

"I was hoping it would be you."

"Excuse me. Have we met?" He vaguely remembered the voice.

"I'm normally in before now. I don't like for anyone to see me, especially at night. Understand that I don't do this just for anyone, so here goes." With that she threw back the hood from her head, revealing beautiful, brown hair that covered her shoulders.

"Of course, you're the melon girl from the market, but why are you so mistrusting of the night?"

"I'm not 'mistrusting' of the night, but my past has left me--- cautious. Do you not remember our last conversation?"

"I remember it all too well. It plagues my thoughts when I get alone, like this, in the moonlight."

"I've been praying for you, Sir. I don't know who you are, but…"

"My friends call me 'Tallow' and you can do the same."

"Well, Tallow, I've been praying that God would reach you."

"Reach me?" Tallow was incredulous.

"Yes. I gathered from before that what you were really looking for (other than Jesus) was peace. Only Jesus can grant you true peace."

"Peace. Oh, you mean turning the other cheek while your enemy wails on your melon."

"No. I mean a peace that can't be won by an enemy bowing under your boot."

"Did she see the games?" Tallow wondered.

"It's a peace acquired not by conquering, but by submitting to Jesus, the Christ. I know true peace from my experience with him."

"Suppose I did give in to this 'Christ' as you called him. Do you know what would happen to me? I'd be marking myself for death."

"Sir…uh Tallow. When you go to war, does the army you're facing not 'mark' you for death?"

"Yes, but in the field you can usually see the enemy coming at you. An assassin's arrow is well hidden."

"Have you even thought of the afterlife? What will happen to your soul once death comes to you?"

"I suppose it'll be a good one. I've been one of Caesar's best men."

"I know that you're a Roman soldier and hold Caesar in high regard, but Caesar has no control over your eternity or his own.

"Watch your words, girl, when speaking of Caesar that way."

"Jesus spoke of his kingdom, but it wasn't an earthly one. His kingdom was one made by God. Even the thief dying next to him believed him, and asked the Lord to remember him when he went there. Jesus promised that very day he would be with him in paradise. Wouldn't you want to live in a place where peace always reigns?"

"You people are all convinced of this 'kingdom' beyond this life where peace is abounding everywhere." Tallow hurled his accusations at Christians. "Think what you will, but I think that anything man is involved in is neither perfect nor peaceful. Even the very best of men have their own agendas to work for."

"I guess you would think that, if you weren't surrendered to the Prince of perfect peace. Sleep well tonight and know that I'm still praying for you."

Tallow waived her off in disgust as she slipped into the night.

*****

The night progressed and Tallow's sleep ran away from him. All the words of Christians haunted his thoughts and echoed to his soul. Out of frustration he yelled out. "What do you want from me?"

He looked around abruptly; knowing that he must've woken the whole garrison. The few that were startled awake thought that he'd stayed too long at the tavern and was crazy drunk.

Tallow decided to continue this outside, away from an audience.

"God…uh Lord…Christ." Tallow stumbled. "I don't know what you've done to all those people in my life, but I do know that their lives are filled with a peace that I wish I felt. I don't know if you can hear this crusted, Roman soldier's prayers, but if you can forgive me of the things I can't forgive myself for, please do." Tallow babbled as his eyes welled up with tears. "Please grant me the peace that those people have. I don't know this 'Christ' that they speak of, but he certainly has changed their lives. I ask that he would change my life as well."

Tallow could feel the peace and forgiveness come over him like nothing he'd ever experienced before. He didn't know how to explain it, but he knew that he was forgiven. He went back to the garrison and drank in peaceful slumber that he'd been missing for years.

Tallow's days and weeks after that night of conversion were not as peaceful for him. He went out of his way to make his killings in the arena as merciful as possible. These efforts were not unnoticed either.

*****

"What makes you hate Tallow so? You've been called names far worse than 'bloodthirsty beast' by some even in the Senate." The room chuckled at Senator Potemus' comment.

"Evidently the good senator doesn't see what the rest of us

do. Your 'lamb champion' is making Rome look bad."

"He's still killing. Is that not what you want?"

"He kills out of defense, not out of attack."

"Excuse me senator, but isn't that what most of the skillful arena kills are, defensive kills? When a man comes at you with a sword, don't you strategize on how to make him not do it again? You cut off the sword hand or put your own through his heart. Wouldn't you say that would stop him, senator?" Potemus embarrassed and angered the senator.

"Let's just put it on the table. I think this 'Tallow' fellow has become a follower of Christ, the one we killed. Remember? He's just keeping up a front because he knows what Rome will do to him. I also heard that while he was in Jerusalem, he inquired of this Christ that we crucified." A dull murmuring filled the room after that statement.

"I have a plan." The senator continued. "Let the lions decide. We can take care of two problems at once. Fill the arena with Christians and turn the beasts loose on them. The sight will make this fellow choose his own fate and we will see where his true allegiance lies."

"Let me warn you, Potemus. If word of this gets to Tallow, the lions will be feasting on your bones as well."

Senator Potemus was backed into a corner and he knew it. He stormed out, stopping at the door to wash his hands and made sure that everyone saw him.

*****

Tallow worked with a wooden mannequin while his father's words haunted him once more. *What makes you think they won't throw Christians into the arena?* He feared for his father and the melon girl.

His blows became a flurry as his feelings welled up inside. His frustration ended with exhaustion. He lifted his eyes to the sky and then looked around.

"God, I don't know what will happen this week or even tomorrow. I ask that you'll give me the strength and the wisdom to do what's right, like my father said. Help me to speak not only with my actions, but with my words for what is good."

*****

Tallow woke to the sound of wooden mannequins clattering. The matches had been posted to take place that afternoon and his friends were sharpening their skills.

The distant moans of hungry lions made him rise to his feet.

"They're hungry for blood, whether it's from man or beast." Kinsmor said ominously.

"I just hope they'll be satisfied after the matches."

"I do as well. Don't get too close to their cage. One of the archers nearly got his arm ripped off this morning."

"What's that archer sharpening his tip for? We aren't going to war, are we?" Tallow questioned.

"It's some special assignment that one of the senators has for them. I don't know what's up, but it's very hush-hush."

"What's the Senate up to?" Tallow thought to himself.

*****

The sun was bearing down as the crowd filtered in to the coliseum. Some of Rome's finest soldiers were mingled in the crowd, dressed in street clothes to not arouse any suspicion.

The announcer's voice echoed throughout the coliseum.

"Friends, countrymen, and citizens of Rome, the matches will begin shortly. First of all, Caesar has a little exercise for your entertainment.

"Not long ago a man came through the Roman Empire speaking of love and forgiveness. He told us to love one another, which was quite a noble task. Rome does not object to loving one another. Aphrodite would applaud you for that." The crowd chuckled.

"When others said that he was king, however, he didn't deny it. Rome has no king but Caesar and we will gladly squash any rebellion that says otherwise. We crucified the man as an example of that."

"Now there is another problem." Tallow's eyes were boring holes into the announcer. "The followers of this 'Christ' are still preaching love and forgiveness, but more treacherous is their belief in 'Christ' as their King. They have even taken his name as their own. Ladies and gentlemen…I give you…the 'Christians' of the Roman Empire."

The crowd erupted in a series of boos and jeers, throwing trash on those who were pushed in front of swords and spears.

"Let's see if your loving God will save you now." The announcer concluded.

Tallow's eyes scanned the crowd in the arena and his fears were realized when they locked onto the melon girl and then his father. The voices from the crowd dulled as the roaring of the lions got closer.

Tallow jerked the spear from an unsuspecting soldier's hand and hurled it into a charging lion. The beast crumbled before reaching its victim. He then leaped from the arena wall, as both blades flashed above his head. He plunged them deep into another lion's neck and with a downward swoop the animal's head fell to the ground. He grabbed the javelin out of the carcass and threw it at a young man's feet.

"Defend your family."

*****

"Sir, do you want me to get more troops in?" A soldier asked the senator.

"No. If the lions don't get him, I've got a special treat for this traitor." He said with a devilish grin.

Tallow saw some familiar faces as his eyes flashed around the arena.

Brutus was pulling an axe from a lion's head while the limp body of another was being tossed off Kinsmor's sword.

The young man with the javelin was keeping two lions at bay while Barsiebus was swinging a rope with a rock on it.

"I'm a bit surprised to see you here." Tallow said as Kinsmor sided with him.

"I liked the odds, besides, you saved my dog." He said, giving his friend a wink.

A woman's scream shot their glances across the arena.

Barsiebus watched with tear filled eyes as the lions ripped the young man apart. He snapped out of the trance and quickly grabbed the spear on a roll and jabbed at the lions. They were more interested in their meal than him now. When the gates were opened, they squabbled over each body part as they went through.

The group in the arena was left alone as the rest of the satisfied lions were herded through the exits.

Tallow couldn't remember the last time he'd cried (as a warrior), but the tears were flowing now at the loss of the innocent.

He waved his sword above his head to get everyone's attention.

"Men of Rome, hear my voice." The crowd's jeers came to a murmur and then silence. "I was brought into the army of Rome as a boy because of my skills in fighting. I grew up in the Roman Army learning various ways to take a man's life from him. I knew nothing of 'Christ' and didn't care to hear about him, until I met one dying soldier. He asked if I 'knew the one he was going to meet?' That intrigued me because he had such confidence in the afterlife." Tallow proceeded to tell of his journey to this very moment in time.

The Senator pulled a captain aside. "Ready the archers! I want this 'Christ' follower to shut up."

"What about the others?" He said pointing to Brutus and Kinsmor.

"They made their choice when they jumped in the arena with him. Let them all die."

Within minutes a tumult of archers all around the coliseum were ready with their weapons.

Tallow saw what was happening and raised his voice even more. "This same Jesus will give you a freedom that can neither be protected nor taken away by anyone. My soul is free despite what may happen here today."

Tallow raised his swords to the sky and crossed them. He then dropped to one knee and flashed a cross of reflected sunlight directly in Caesar's face.

His two comrades looked at each other and snapped into a fighting stance.

The archers' bows were bent to almost the breaking point when a distant voice growled. "Shoot your weapons!"

The arena floor soon turned white as arrows were splintered and thrown to the ground by the fury of Tallow's blades.

Brutus and Kinsmor were cut down early by the storm of raining arrows. The others in the arena shortly followed them to the ground.

With a lull in the firing Tallow relaxed a bit. It was then that Grayboe saw his target. His eyes filled with tears as he released the arrow from his bow.

Tallow arched his back as the arrow pierced his side. Instantly, other arrows followed from every direction as the great warrior kneeled.

Tallow's grimacing face soon faded as he looked to the heavens. A serene smile appeared at the sight of his Savior. The one Tallow had searched for so long, was standing with open arms waiting for Tallow to come. With his last bit of strength, Tallow stretched his arms toward heaven and collapsed.

So is the story of Tallow. It is the story of a boy who became so much more than a warrior and a gladiator. He became a true champion.

Authors Bio

Scott Risch grew up and currently resides in South Texas. He enjoyed the artistic side of school. Scott, enjoys lounging in the back yard and writing about the adventuress critters he observes. Scott and his wife Karyn, currently reside in Pearland, Texas. Karyn, a pre-Kindergarten teacher is an excellent source of encouragement and kid knowledge.

Other Titles by Scott Risch

Title: Squirrel Chronicles
- Author: Scott Risch
- Publisher: Mouse Gate Press
- Paper Back: ISBN: 9781590951231
- eBook: ISBN: 9781648835087
- Number of pages: 100
- Publication Date: 2020

Squirrel Chronicles tells the adventures of a squirrel named Smokey and his buddy Ringer. In their experiences, these two young squirrels learn life lessons, friendship, loving your enemies, and most importantly the love of the Creator.

Parents, teachers, librarians, and kids will appreciate the worldwide geography and appropriate language for Ages 6–10 Grades: 1–5.